T O O L

MW00976850

Plant and Prune

Patty Whitehouse

ROURKE
PUBLISHING

www.rourkepublishing.com

www.rourkepublishing.com

PHOTO CREDITS: © Craig Lopetz: pages 4, 5, 7, 19; © Armentrout: pages 6, 8, 9, 10, 11, 12, 13, 14, 16, 17; © PIR: page 15; © mattsson: page 20; © Stan Rohver: page 21; © lisafx: page 22

Editor: Robert Stengard-Olliges

Cover design by Nicola Stratford

Library of Congress Cataloging-in-Publication Data

Whitehouse, Patricia, 1958-
  Plant and prune / Patty Whitehouse.
      p. cm. -- (Tool kit)
  Includes index.
  ISBN 978-1-60044-210-0 (hardcover)
  ISBN 978-1-59515-565-8 (softcover)
  ISBN 978-1-60472-059-4 (Lap Book)
  ISBN 978-1-60472-119-5 (eBook)
  1. Garden tools--Juvenile literature. 2. Gardening--Juvenile literature.
I. Title. II. Series: Whitehouse, Patricia, 1958- Tool kit.

SB454.8.W48 2007
631.3--dc22

2006010735

Rourke Publishing
Printed in the United States of America, North Mankato, Minnesota
030411
030411LP-B

www.rourkepublishing.com - rourke@rourkepublishing.com
Post Office Box 643328 Vero Beach, Florida 32964

Table of Contents

Working In The Garden

Here is a **garden**. The plants in the garden need water. The **soil** needs to be **tilled**.

People will water and till the garden, but they will use **tools** when they work.

Growing Things

Tools help with many kinds of work. Tools make work easier and faster.

Tools in this book help people grow things. People who use them are **gardeners**.

Spading Forks, Claws and Hoes

Some tools break apart soil. Gardeners use a spading fork for big areas. They use a hand claw for small areas.

A hoe breaks up soil around small plants. The **blade** on a hoe also pulls out small **weeds**.

Spreaders

Some seeds are hard to plant. Gardeners use a spreader to spread grass seed on the soil.

Some plants need **fertilizer** to grow. This spreader puts fertilizer in the right places.

Shovels, Trowels, and Spades

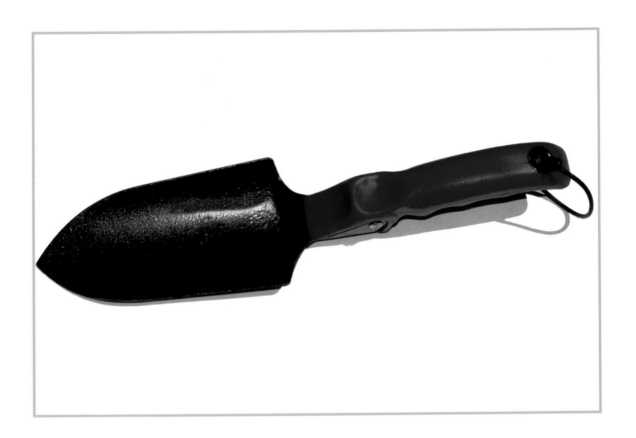

A shovel has a **scooped** blade. Gardeners use shovels to dig holes. A hand shovel is called a trowel.

A spade has a flat blade. Gardeners use spades and shovels to dig up and move soil.

Rakes

A rake is a garden tool with **tines**. A bow rake has short tines for moving soil.

A fan rake has long tines. Gardeners use it to rake leaves.

Watering Cans and Sprinklers

Plants need water to grow. Gardeners use watering cans to water the garden.

A sprinkler hooks up to a hose. When the water is on,
it sprays through the holes in the sprinkler.

Pruning Shears and Hedge Trimmers

Gardeners need to trim some plants. Pruning shears look like scissors. They cut small stems.

Hedge trimmers are much bigger. Gardeners need
two hands to use them. They cut big stems.

Machines In The Garden

This is a rototill. It mixes up the soil. Now the soil is ready to grow plants.

This is a lawn mower. It uses gasoline to make it work. Blades on the lawnmower spin around to cut the grass.

Be Safe With Tools

You should have an adult help you with any tools. You should wear gloves and goggles to protect yourself.

GLOSSARY

blade (BLAYD) — sharp part of a tool

fertilizer (FUR tuh li zer) — plant food

garden (GARD uhn) — place where plants grow

gardener (GAR duh ner) — person who works in a garden

scooped (SKOOPD) — rounded or bent

soil (SOYL) — top layer of earth where plants grow

till (TIL) — to get the soil ready for planting

tine (TINE) — one pointed part of a rake

tool (TOOL) — something that helps people do work

weed (WEED) — an unwanted plant

INDEX

FURTHER READING

Auch, Alison J. *Garden Tools.* Compass Point Books:
   Minneapolis, MN, 2003.
Henderson, Kathy. *And The Good Brown Earth.* Candlewick Press:
   Boston, 2004.
Snyder, Inez. *Gardening Tools.* Children's Press: New York, 2002.

WEBSITES TO VISIT

www.urbanext.uiuc.edu/firstgarden/
www.homeandgardensite.com/ChildrensSite/index.htm

ABOUT THE AUTHOR

Patty Whitehouse has been a teacher for 17 years. She is currently a Lead Science teacher in Chicago, where she lives with her husband and two teenage children. She enjoys reading, gardening, and writing about science for children.